MYSTERY
AT THE MASKED BALL

Look for these books in the
Clue™ series:

MYSTERY
AT THE MASKED BALL

Book created by A. E. Parker

Written by Eric Weiner

Based on characters from the Parker Brothers game

A Creative Media Applications Production

SCHOLASTIC INC.
New York Toronto London Auckland Sydney

*Special thanks to: Thomas Dusenberry,
Julie Ryan, Laura Millhollin, Jean Feiwel,
Greg Holch, Dona Smith, Nancy Smith,
John Simko, and Elizabeth Parisi.*

ISBN 0-590-45633-4

24 23 22 21 20 19 18 17 16 15 14 13   6   7/9

Printed in the U.S.A.   40

First Scholastic printing, February 1993

For Mrs. Jeffreys, Mrs. Schreiber,
and Miss Tomaisson

Contents

MYSTERY
AT THE MASKED BALL

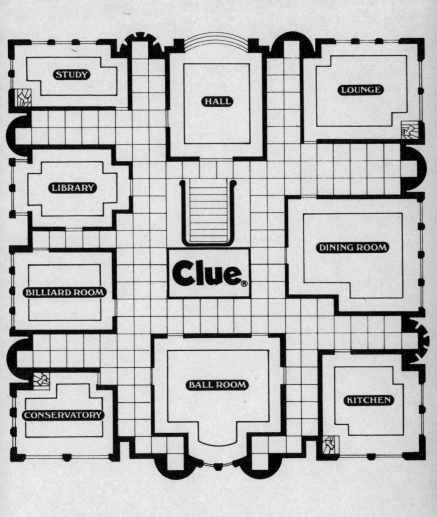

Allow Me to Introduce Myself . . .

MY NAME IS REGINALD BODDY, THE owner of this mansion — and your host. I trust that you'll have a pleasant, peaceful visit. At least, let's hope no one gets murdered!

As you may remember, the last time you were here, my guests all shot me. Well, lucky for me, they loaded their guns with my trick rainbow-colored bullets — the kind that pierce everything except human skin. Whew! They nearly scared me to death. What pranksters!

I had the last laugh, though. *They* thought the bullets were real. Ha-ha-ha!

Anyway!

While you're here, I'd like to ask you a favor. Look for clues, would you? Not that I think my guests are going to commit any crimes. But if they *do*, I'd love it if you would solve them for me.

You have only six suspects to worry about. (I, of course, will never be a suspect!) The six suspects are:

Mr. Green: a kind-hearted fellow who would

never hurt a flea. But if you're not a flea, you'd better watch out.

Colonel Mustard: A gallant, dashing man — always *dashing* off to a duel.

Mrs. Peacock: If only she'd mind her own business as strictly as she minds her manners!

Professor Plum: He's invented loads of things — if only he could remember some of them!

Miss Scarlet: Perhaps Miss Scarlet isn't vain — maybe she just likes mirrors!

Mrs. White: My loyal maid doesn't have a violent bone in her body. But she has lots of violent weapons, so be careful.

Don't worry — I'll give you a chart of the suspects, weapons, and rooms at the end of each mystery. As you read, you can check off the lists until you've narrowed your list down to one suspect, weapon, and room.

What's that? You want to know why I'm holding a Revolver? And why Mr. Green's corpse is lying at my feet? You know, those are both excellent questions.

AYYYYYYYYYYYYYYYYYYY!!!!

1.
Mr. Boddy Kills a Guest

MR. BODDY STOOD IN THE LOUNGE, HIS face twisted in horror. In his hand was a Revolver. At his feet lay Mr. Green.

"AYYYYYYYYYYYYYYYYYYYY!!!!" Boddy screamed.

Mrs. White, his maid, hurried into the room carrying a crystal punch bowl. "Yes, sir, you called for me?" she asked.

Then she saw Mr. Green and she screamed, too. The crystal punch bowl fell from her grasp and shattered at her feet.

"What happened?" Mr. Boddy asked her in a daze.

"I dropped the punch bowl," answered Mrs. White.

"Before that," said Boddy.

"You shot Mr. Green," Mrs. White replied.

"I was afraid you'd say that," sighed Mr. Boddy. "This is all so very, very strange. You see, I can't remember a thing. I *certainly* can't remember shooting anyone. You believe me, don't you?"

"Of course I believe you," nodded Mrs. White. Then she turned her back and mouthed the word, "Not!"

"Why would I shoot Mr. Green?" wondered the stunned Mr. Boddy. "I have no motive!" Then Mr. Boddy noticed something in his right hand. Mr. Green's stuffed wallet!

"Well, there's your motive," said the maid. "You wanted his money so you robbed him and killed him."

"But I didn't," sputtered Boddy. "Why would I want his money? I'm a billionaire, a zillionaire, a gazillionaire! Not only that, I'm rich!"

"It certainly was greedy of you," commented Mrs. White.

"Please, Mrs. White," begged Boddy. "Tell me everything that happened in the last five minutes. Maybe something will jog my memory."

"Let's see," said Mrs. White. "Five minutes ago . . . that was when Mr. Green got here. He was the first of your weekend guests to arrive at the mansion. I told him that you were in the Lounge, and sent him in."

"Yes, yes," said Boddy. "I remember he came in here. But I have amnesia about everything that happened next."

The doorbell began ringing.

"The doorbell," said Mrs. White.

"Yes, the doorbell," murmured Boddy. "That rings a bell. Thank you for reminding me."

4

"No," said the maid. "The doorbell is really ringing. Someone's at the door."

They rushed to the front door. There stood Miss Scarlet, dressed up in a bright red dress with a red feather boa, red purse, and blue gloves. "What's up?" she asked.

"Everything is fine," lied Mrs. White. "Except Mr. Boddy just shot Mr. Green."

"I didn't! I didn't!" insisted Boddy. Clutching his head, he ran from the doorway weeping.

Right smack into the yellow-gloved hands of — Professor Plum.

"How did you get in, Professor Plum?" Mrs. White demanded. "I certainly didn't let you in."

"I arrived earlier and found the front door open," Plum explained. "I've been snoozing in the Billiard Room ever since."

"Well, you sure are a sound sleeper," said Miss Scarlet. "You slept right through a murder. Our host has just shot Mr. Green."

"Please don't say that," begged Boddy. "I'm innocent. I just can't remember what happened."

"Getting forgetful, eh?" said the Professor. "Well, I know what that's like — if I haven't forgotten."

The doorbell rang again.

"The doorbell," murmured Boddy once more, remembering something.

This time it was Mrs. Peacock. "Mr. Boddy," she gushed. "It's been too long, hasn't it?"

5

"I don't know," said Boddy to himself. "I can't remember."

The blue peacock feather in Mrs. Peacock's hat began to quiver. Mrs. Peacock was shaking with rage. "How rude!"

"He means he can't remember why he just murdered Mr. Green," explained Miss Scarlet.

"He just murdered Mr. Green?" exclaimed Mrs. Peacock. "Even ruder!"

"Oh, please help me!" Boddy pleaded with all his guests.

Mrs. Peacock thought for a moment. "Why don't we return to the scene of the crime?" she suggested. "Maybe that will help shock you out of your amnesia." Placing a blue-gloved hand firmly on Boddy's shoulder, Mrs. Peacock led everyone back to the Lounge — where they stared at the body of Mr. Green. Suddenly, Boddy cried out, "I remember something! I remember that I was standing by that dresser when this all began."

"Doing what?" Mrs. White asked.

"Combing my hair in the mirror," Boddy further recalled.

"Fascinating," said Plum, who had forgotten what all the fuss was about.

"Here's the comb," said Mrs. Peacock.

"And there's the mirror," added Miss Scarlet, glancing at her reflection.

"So far, so good," said Mrs. Peacock. "Go on,

Mr. Boddy. Try to think back. What happened then?"

"Then," said Boddy, "then . . . the doorbell rang."

The doorbell rang.

Boddy screamed.

"It's just the front door again," Mrs. White assured him. She sneered as she hurried out of the Lounge.

"Sorry," said Boddy. But then he screamed again. "I just remembered something else. I saw a face in the mirror as I was combing my hair. But I can't remember what face!"

The guests exchanged glances. "Usually, one sees one's *own* face in the mirror," Miss Scarlet spoke up.

"No, no, no!" cried Mr. Boddy impatiently. There was *another* face, too!"

Mr. Boddy stared into the mirror, trying to remember. Suddenly, he turned pale and started to shake.

The other face had appeared in the mirror all over again.

It was Colonel Mustard's face.

Mr. Boddy whirled around. "How did you get in here, Colonel Mustard?" demanded Mr. Boddy.

"I let him in," said Mrs. White, entering behind Mustard.

"But you were here earlier, Colonel," accused Mrs. Peacock, "weren't you? Weren't you?"

"So I was," said the Colonel, stepping over the body of Mr. Green. "What of it?"

"So maybe you're the one who murdered Mr. Green," said Miss Scarlet.

"With what?" asked Mustard. He held out his yellow-gloved hands. "I don't have a weapon. I gave my Revolver to Mr. Boddy for safekeeping. Then I went for a walk."

Mr. Boddy staggered to the sofa and collapsed.

"Come on," said Mrs. Peacock. "Try to remember what happened after Mustard gave you his Revolver for safekeeping."

"Um, then Mr. Green came in," mumbled Mr. Boddy. "And he gave me his wallet for safekeeping, just like Mustard did with the gun. And while I was talking to him, the Revolver went off. But I wasn't the one who pulled the trigger!"

"Never mind about that," said Mrs. Peacock. "Just keep remembering. What happened next?"

"And then Mr. Green . . . fell to the floor . . . dead!"

"Hmm. That awful sight must have been the shock that gave you your amnesia," mused Peacock. "You know, I'm beginning to think you didn't commit this crime after all. Look, everyone. The door to the secret passageway from the Lounge to the Conservatory is open."

"What's that got to do with anything?" asked Plum.

"Well, what if someone was standing in the se-

8

cret doorway, behind Mr. Boddy?" Mrs. Peacock asked. "They're about to enter the room, right? But then they see Boddy pointing the gun at Green. 'Aha!' thinks our killer. 'I've got a chance to kill Mr. Green and get away with it, because everyone will think it was Mr. Boddy who did it.' "

Mrs. Peacock stared down at Mr. Green's lifeless body. "I liked Mr. Green, myself," she said. "But I'm sure there were a lot of people who wouldn't be able to resist such a perfect opportunity to do him in."

"Well, *I'm* innocent," said Miss Scarlet, tossing her red feather boa over her shoulder. "I didn't even arrive at the mansion until after Mr. Green was murdered."

"Not true," said Mrs. Peacock. "Because I saw you tiptoeing through the Kitchen ten minutes before the murder!"

"That's a lie!" screamed Miss Scarlet. "I wasn't here. I swear it!"

"It's not a lie!" said Professor Plum. "When I heard the gunshots, I opened my eyes and I, too, saw Miss Scarlet tiptoeing by."

"All right, all right, I was here," admitted Miss Scarlet. "But the only reason I was tiptoeing around was that I didn't want to wake up Professor Plum. I saw he was napping. When I couldn't find Mr. Boddy or Mrs. White, I decided I had arrived too early. Like the Colonel, I went for a walk."

"A highly suspicious story," said Mrs. Peacock.

Suddenly, Mr. Boddy sat bolt upright on the sofa and cried, "Wait!"

There was a look of fresh terror in his eyes. "I remember it now!" he said. "It was so horrible I blocked it out!"

"What?" asked all the guests at once.

"I remember I sensed something just before the shot rang out. I glanced over my shoulder and saw . . ."

The guests all stamped their feet with impatience. "Saw what?!"

"I saw a blue-gloved hand that slowly stuck out of the secret passageway. It was pointing a Revolver."

"So I was right!" cried Mrs. Peacock.

"Think!" cried Miss Scarlet, rushing to Boddy's side. "Can you picture the murderer's face?"

Mr. Boddy thought and thought. Then he fell back on the sofa. "No," he gasped. "I just can't remember any more."

WHO KILLED MR. GREEN?

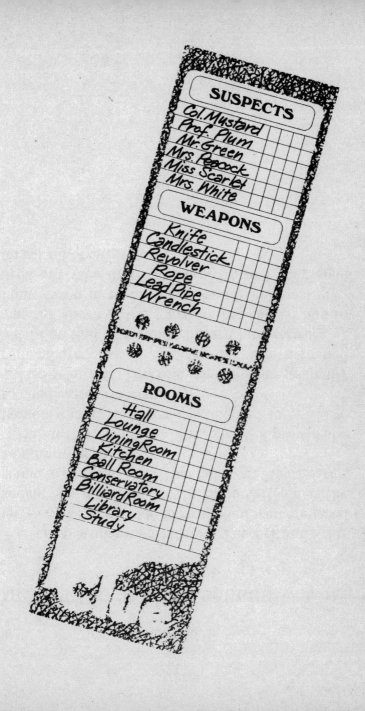

SOLUTION

MRS. PEACOCK in the LOUNGE with the REVOLVER

Of the possible suspects, only Peacock and Scarlet were wearing blue gloves. Plum remembered seeing Scarlet tiptoe by the Billiard Room at the sound of the gunshots. That rules out Miss Scarlet as a murder suspect.

But at the same time, Mrs. Peacock proved she herself was at the mansion. She had to be there to see Scarlet tiptoeing by.

Lucky for Mrs. Peacock, when the guests finally remembered to call a doctor, Mr. Green turned out to be fine. The bullet missed him entirely. It was the shock of the gunshot that caused him to faint. Even more luckily, none of the guests figured out who fired the revolver, and they soon forgot all about it.

2.
Pick a Pocket, Any Pocket

"**A**ND NOW," SAID MR. BODDY IN THE Ball Room, "allow me to present our speaker for today.

"Let's have a big round of applause for . . . Mr. Green."

Mr. Boddy clapped loudly. Mr. Green clapped even louder. Then he crossed to the chalkboard and picked up a piece of green chalk. "Ways to Get Rich," he wrote.

Just then the Ball Room door swung open. "Mr. Boddy," Mrs. White called. "Your mail." She presented Boddy with an envelope on a silver tray.

Mr. Boddy opened the envelope and pulled out a card. "Why, it's from my Aunt Augusta. Wishing me a happy birthday."

The guests gasped. "Oh, no! Did we forget your birthday?"

Mr. Boddy smiled. "Not at all. I'm afraid Aunt Augusta is getting on in years, and getting a little absentminded. My birthday isn't for another 365 days."

"Fine," said Green, stamping his feet. "Now do you mind if we get started?"

"Sorry," said Boddy, pocketing the card.

But at that moment, something came out of the card. It fluttered to the ground. It was green.

Mr. Boddy bent down to pick it up. "Now isn't that special!" he cooed. "Look what Aunt Augusta sent me!" He held up a crisp new $100 bill.

All of the guests smiled warmly. Several guests drooled. Boddy quickly folded up the bill and stuffed it in his breast pocket.

"Let's get *going*!" shrieked Mr. Green, turning purple.

Professor Plum spoke up. "I don't know how to get rich," he began. "But I can tell you how *not* to do it. I invested in an umbrella company right before a big drought. Ha-ha-ha!" He cleared his throat. "By the way, I wonder if anyone could lend me some money?"

Miss Scarlet pulled out a red beaded purse. She handed the professor two crisp $100 bills.

"Gee, thanks," said Plum.

"Listen, would it be too much to ask to have everyone's attention up here?" Green barked.

Everyone looked at Green. That gave Mrs. Peacock a chance to pickpocket one of Plum's $100 bills.

"Well, can anyone give us any ideas on how to get rich?" asked Mr. Green.

Plum had an idea. But he kept it to himself. He

14

pickpocketed two $100 bills from Mrs. Peacock.

"You could inherit the money," called out Mr. Boddy.

"Inherit," repeated Green, writing down the answer. "Very good answer. The only problem is, if you don't have rich relatives, then you're kind of out of luck, aren't you? Can anyone think of another way?"

"Well," said Mrs. Peacock, "you could write a book." She opened her blue valise and pulled out several copies of a thick book titled, *The Proper Way to Be Proper*. "The price is proper, too," she added. "Only $100."

"Sold!" cried Plum.

"I'll take a copy, too," said Miss Scarlet.

Both she and the professor handed Mrs. Peacock crisp new $100 bills.

"Okay, good," said Green. "Write a book." He wrote the suggestion on the blackboard. "Any other ideas?"

Miss Scarlet raised her hand. "I've started a company to sell my own line of red lipstick. It's called 'Simply Scarlet.'" She pulled a tube of bright red lipstick from her pocket and showed everyone.

"I'll invest $100," announced Mrs. Peacock, handing over a smooth $100 bill.

"And I'll invest $300," said Mrs. White, handing over three new $100 bills.

"If you're finished," growled Green. "Can any-

15

one suggest one more way to get rich? Anyone? Anyone?"

The guests thought and thought. Mr. Boddy thought so hard that beads of sweat popped out on his forehead. He reached in his breast pocket for his handkerchief.

Except, there was no handkerchief.

That didn't bother him so much. But something else wasn't in his pocket either. "Er," he said. "I'm sorry to interrupt, and I certainly don't want to make a fuss, but it seems I've been . . . well . . . robbed."

"What?" cried Green. "This is an outrage! Everyone empty their pockets at once."

The guests all did as they were told.

Mrs. Peacock pulled out a fan, a bobby pin, a nickel, a penny, a crisp $100 bill, and a chocolate-chip cookie.

Mustard pulled out a wad of sticky gum, a monocle, a Revolver, a mustache trimmer, three crumpled twenties, a ripped five, a creased $100 bill, and six shiny pennies.

Professor Plum pulled out two new $100 bills, a purple yo-yo, and a phone bill from three months ago. "No wonder they cut off my service," said the surprised professor.

Mrs. White pulled out a Revolver, a Knife, a Lead Pipe, a Wrench, and three new $100 bills. "I found the weapons while I was cleaning up," she explained with an innocent shrug.

Miss Scarlet pulled out a mirror, red eye shadow, a box of hot candies, and four brand-new $100 bills.

"Hmm," said a puzzled Mr. Boddy. "Looks like any one of you could have taken it."

"All right," said Mustard. "Who's got the sticky fingers?"

"You do," Plum said, pointing to the gum stuck to Mustard's fingers.

"No," said the Colonel. "I meant, who took Boddy's money?"

WHO STOLE BODDY'S $100 BILL?

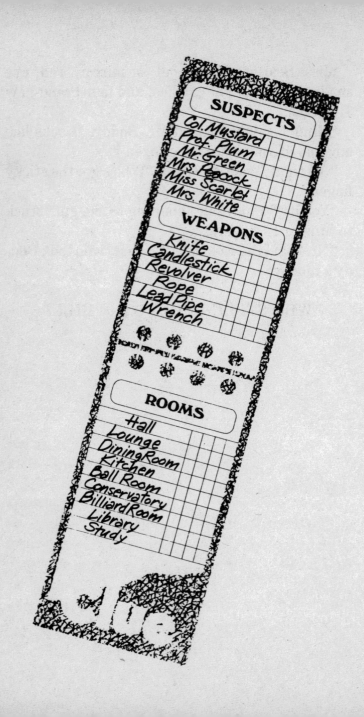

SOLUTION

COLONEL MUSTARD in the BALL ROOM

Boddy folded up his bill before pocketing it. Only Mustard's $100 bill was creased. And since he didn't exchange any money with the other guests, he must be the original thief.

Mr. Boddy was very annoyed until Mustard explained that he was just trying to demonstrate a fourth way of getting rich.

3.
A Tug-of-War

"GRIP THE ROPE!" YELLED MR. BODDY.

Five guests and Mr. Boddy's maid gripped the Rope with all their might for a game of tug-of-war.

One team of three people faced the other team of three people.

Mr. Boddy raised his Revolver. "You all know the rules," he called. "When the last member of one team has been dragged across this white line, then the tug-of-war is over. I will award the winning team a rare Boddy treasure. May the best team win."

Boddy fired.

The tug-of-war was on. Both teams grunted, groaned, moaned, and wailed. They dug their feet into Boddy's green lawn. Grass and dirt flew everywhere. The players tugged, jerked, pulled, and yanked with all their might.

The Rope began to move. First it was only an inch. But soon the inch became a foot. The Rope was moving steadily to the left.

"Stop them! Pull back!" Mustard shouted desperately.

"I'm pulling as hard as I can," Plum wheezed back over his shoulder as he gave a tremendous tug.

"We're still winning!" Mrs. Peacock cried to the other team as the rope moved left.

Directly across from her, Miss Scarlet sneered, "No way, Peacock!"

Sure enough, the Rope started moving right.

Then left again. Then right.

Mr. Boddy swiveled his head back and forth. The fight kept seesawing.

Finally, Mr. Green was dragged — kicking and screaming — across the white line. Again Boddy fired off his Revolver.

"That's the match," he said. "And the winner is — "

WHO WON?
AND WHAT WERE THE POSITIONS OF ALL
THE PLAYERS?

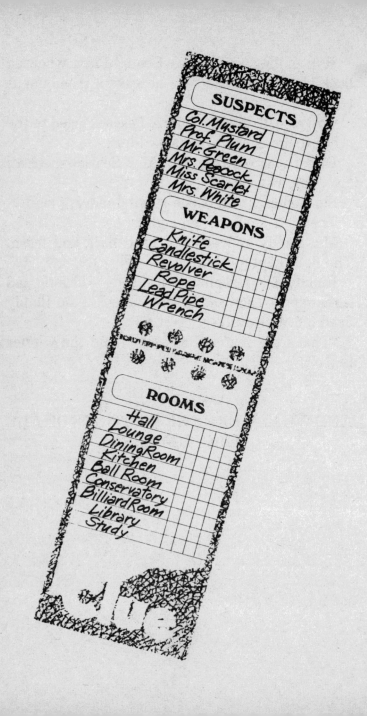

SOLUTION

MR. GREEN, MRS. WHITE, and MRS. PEA-COCK versus MISS SCARLET, PROFESSOR PLUM, and COLONEL MUSTARD. SCARLET, PLUM, and MUSTARD's team won.

When the Rope began moving left, Mustard yelled desperately at Plum to pull. Mustard and Plum were on the right, then. And Plum, we learn, was ahead of Mustard.

In the next exchange, we see that Mrs. Peacock was excited about the Rope moving left, and that Miss Scarlet was facing her. That means that on the right were Scarlet, Plum, and Mustard, in that order. And on the left were Green and Mrs. White (we don't yet know in what order), with Mrs. Peacock leading the way.

Boddy had said that the tug-of-war would end when the last member of a team was dragged across the white line. When Green crossed the line, Boddy fired his Revolver to end the match. So Green was the last player on the left. That means that Mrs. White must have been second.

By the way, Mr. Boddy kept his promise. He gave each member of the winning team a rare Boddy treasure — a big kiss on the nose.

4.
The Deadly Toothbrush

RED RUBIES COVERED THE HANDLE OF the deadly toothbrush.

The toothbrush gleamed. It glowed. It had been in Miss Scarlet's family for generations, and it was deadly because people had murdered for the chance to possess its wealth.

Miss Scarlet was trying to squeeze toothpaste onto the bristles.

But the ruby light was just too dazzling. Miss Scarlet couldn't see what she was doing. She squeezed toothpaste all over her red silk pajamas.

"Phooey!" she grumbled. "Just what I don't need. And Mrs. White is out of town and won't be able to clean them for me. Phooey!"

As she spoke, Mrs. Peacock entered. "Phooey!" was not the greeting she had expected. "How rude!" she cried.

"I wasn't talking to you," Miss Scarlet said.

"Even ruder!" gasped Peacock. Then she looked at Miss Scarlet suspiciously. "What are you doing in the Billiard Room, anyway? Shouldn't you be in one of the guest rooms?"

"My bed's too soft," Miss Scarlet explained. "I'm going to sleep on the pool table."

"Oh." Mrs. Peacock nodded. Then she blinked. Then she gaped. "Are those *real* jewels on your toothbrush?"

"Of course," said Miss Scarlet, turning red.

"How vulgar!" said Mrs. Peacock. "Good night!" She strode angrily out of the room.

Miss Scarlet sighed. She squeezed some more toothpaste onto the ruby toothbrush, then headed down the hallway to the nearest bathroom.

She didn't get there. As she rounded the corner, she smacked right into Mr. Green.

The toothpaste on the ruby toothbrush splattered all over Mr. Green's green nightshirt.

Mr. Green didn't notice. He was staring at the toothbrush. The deadly toothbrush.

"Are those real rubies?"

"Uh huh. Now if you don't mind — "

Miss Scarlet tried to get past Green but he blocked her way. "Listen," he sneered, "can I borrow that toothbrush?"

"I never share toothbrushes," snapped Miss Scarlet. And she hurried on to the bathroom.

But she never got there.

As she rounded the next corner, she smacked right into Colonel Mustard.

"En garde!" screamed Mustard. "Prepare to fight!" Then he recognized Miss Scarlet and relaxed. "Are you crazy?" he demanded. "You could have been killed!"

"Sorry," said Miss Scarlet. "I was just in a hurry to get to the bathroom."

Colonel Mustard wasn't listening. He was staring at the toothbrush. The deadly toothbrush. "Are those — "

"Real rubies?" Miss Scarlet was getting used to this question. "Yes, but you can't borrow it. Good night!"

She hurried on to the bathroom. The door was locked.

"Is someone in there?" Miss Scarlet called.

"I forget," Professor Plum called back.

Miss Scarlet waited. She waited a long time. Finally, the door opened. "Sorry I took so long," said Plum. "I couldn't remember why I was in there."

The Professor's mouth dropped open. He was staring at the toothbrush. The deadly toothbrush.

"That's it!" he cried. "Now I remember!" He removed a purple toothbrush from the breast pocket of his purple pajamas. He rushed back into the bathroom and slammed the door.

Two hours later . . .

*　　*　　*

Two hours later, Colonel Mustard was still awake.

He was fighting an imaginary duel in his head.

"Take *that*, you scoundrel!" he snarled suddenly at his make-believe opponent.

He whirled and whipped the silver Wrench out of the mustard-yellow pocket of his pajamas.

Except his palms were sweaty with nervousness and he whipped the Wrench right out the open window.

"Blast!" Mustard muttered.

He trudged outside to fetch his Wrench, carefully leaving the front door ajar behind him.

Just as his hand closed on the Wrench, he heard a loud noise.

Was it a shotgun blast?

Mustard looked around wildly.

Then he saw what had happened.

A gust of wind had slammed the front door of the mansion shut with a loud slam.

"Aggghh!" Colonel Mustard cried, as he ran barefoot across the cold lawn. Sure enough, the door was now locked. He reached for the knocker. Then he remembered. It was the middle of the night. If he knocked he would disturb the whole mansion.

"Perhaps someone is still awake," he told himself. He stepped off the porch. And fell right into the bramble bush.

"I shall lose my temper in a minute," Mustard told himself when he finally thrashed his way out of the bush. Then he saw something which cheered him up immensely. Mrs. Peacock's window was still lit.

"Good old Mrs. Peacock," he said warmly as he peered through the window.

Mrs. Peacock peered back.

"A prowler!" she shrieked. Then she fired.

This time, he knew it was a real shotgun blast. It blasted the tassel right off Mustard's yellow nightcap.

"Have you gone crazy?" he shrieked, running away.

Mrs. Peacock, meanwhile, was busy locking and barring her door with all the heavy furniture in her room. Then she went back to bed and stayed there for the rest of the night.

There was nothing for Mustard to do but try to waken someone else.

He searched the ground until he found a pebble. Then he threw it at Plum's dark window. It hit the glass with a light tap.

There was no response from Plum. Mustard tried a larger pebble. Then a big rock.

Just before the big rock hit Plum's window, Plum opened the window and looked outside. "Who's there?" he asked. Then he was knocked unconscious by the rock.

"Sorry about that," Mustard called.

Just then, lightning struck. It began to pour. Mustard shivered miserably in the cold rain.

There was no way around it, he decided. He would have to knock on the front door after all and wake up everyone in the mansion. Everyone except poor Plum, that is.

But just then a light snapped on in the Billiard Room, and Colonel Mustard saw something terrible. He saw the silhouette of Miss Scarlet being attacked from behind by a hand holding a Candlestick as a club!

Mustard screamed out a warning — but it was no use. Miss Scarlet fell. The hand disappeared. Then it briefly reappeared again. Now the silhouette of a hand was holding something new.

It was holding the silhouette of a toothbrush. The deadly toothbrush.

WHO CLUBBED MISS SCARLET?

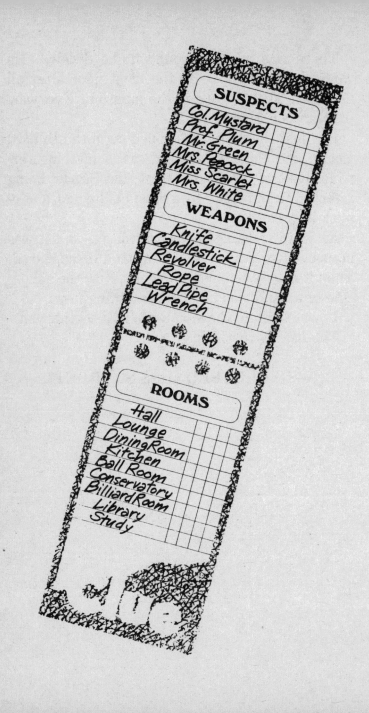

SOLUTION

MR. GREEN in the BILLIARD ROOM with the CANDLESTICK

We can rule out Mrs. Peacock, who locked herself in her room and went back to bed. Plum was unconscious. Mustard was outside. Mrs. White was out of town.

That leaves Mr. Green.

Lucky for Plum and Scarlet, they both survived with only bad headaches.

Lucky for Green, he got away with his crime. But because he never used the ruby toothbrush, he had six cavities at his next checkup.

5.
The Hobby Club

PROFESSOR PLUM WALKED FROM THE Library to the Hall to the Study. He strolled through the secret passageway to the Kitchen. He hurried to the Ball Room. He *ran* to the Conservatory. And after glancing at his watch, he raced through the secret passageway to the Lounge.

There he found Mr. Boddy, Mrs. White, and the four other guests. "Ah," he said, snapping his fingers. "The Lounge! Right! That's where the meeting was being held."

Mr. Boddy smiled. "Don't worry, Professor. Our Hobby Club meeting is just under way. We're taking turns announcing our new hobbies."

"I have a new hobby," Plum announced with a smile. "Memory tricks!"

Everyone guffawed. Plum turned purple.

"I know," he said. "Sometimes I can be a little forgetful. That's why I thought this would be a perfect hobby for me. Look," he said, holding up an empty hand. "I found this book in the mansion Library. *Ten Days to a Better Memory.*"

"In your case it should say ten *years*," joked Mustard. "You've forgotten the book."

Plum stared at his hand in confusion. Then he said, "Right. Excuse me a moment, would you?"

And he was gone.

"Poor Professor Plum," said Miss Scarlet, standing on her tippy-toes. "Do you think he'll ever learn to be less absentminded?"

"Let's see," said Mrs. Peacock, flipping a penny. "Heads says he never will. . . . Heads it is!"

"Is that your new hobby?" asked Mr. Boddy. "Telling the future?"

"No," said Mrs. Peacock. "Coin collecting. See?" She held up the penny.

"You're off to a great start," said Mr. Green. "That collection must be worth, oh, at least two cents!"

When the members of the Hobby Club stopped laughing, Mrs. Peacock said, "Actually, it's worth $100,000."

Five jaws dropped open.

"No way!" said Mrs. White.

"Way!" replied Mrs. Peacock.

Mustard pulled out a pocketful of change. "Then I'm a millionaire," he said. "I've got ten pennies."

"Yes," said Mrs. Peacock. "But if you'll allow me." She took one of Mustard's pennies.

"Now you owe me $100,000," Mustard joked.

"I'm afraid not. Look at the difference between the two pennies. See how on my penny, Lincoln

33

is upside-down? He's standing on his head, you might say. It's a mistake. And it's the only upside-down penny that's ever been found. That's what makes it so valuable."

The Hobby Club let out one long whistle — and one hum. Mr. Green was playing Beethoven's Fifth Symphony on his kazoo (his new hobby).

"And now," said Mrs. Peacock, "if you'll excuse me, I've got to do some standing on my head myself. Yoga, as you'll remember, is my other hobby."

"But the meeting isn't over," said Mr. Boddy. "Don't you want to hear everyone else's new hobby?"

"All right," said Mrs. Peacock. "I'll stay. Even though you all laughed at me."

"Oh now, we didn't laugh at you," said the guests. "We . . ."

But they couldn't think of anything else to say. They *had* laughed at her, after all.

"Mr. Green? What's your hobby?" said Boddy.

In response, Mr. Green hummed several bars on his kazoo.

Mustard covered his ears with his hands.

Green turned green. With his red-sneakered foot, he kicked Mustard in the shin.

Mustard wanted to challenge Green to a duel, but Miss Scarlet stepped between them.

"Stop it and watch me," she said. Then she leaped across the room, landed flat on her red sneakers, stood on her tippy-toes, twirled, spun, jumped, and bowed. "Can you guess my hobby?"

There was silence in the room.

Miss Scarlet turned scarlet. "Ballet!" she snapped.

There was a strange beeping. Everyone looked at Mrs. White. She was holding a small video game. "My new hobby is going to be Kunga-Dunga," she explained, as the game beeped again. Then an electronic voice said, "Kunga-Dunga! You lose!"

The guests all rolled their eyes.

"My new hobby's moth collecting," said Mustard. He pulled out a butterfly net and swiped it at a moth fluttering by. He missed, but he conked Boddy on the head.

Mrs. Peacock stood up. "Well, now I *am* going to leave. I still have to do my yoga exercises. I need a hard floor and a room where I won't be disturbed. Mr. Boddy, mind if I use the — "

She stopped. The other members of the Hobby Club were all staring and listening, hard.

Mrs. Peacock whispered the name of the room in Boddy's ear.

"Not at all," said Boddy. "Go right ahead. I promise you I won't disturb you."

"Neither will we," promised the rest of the Hobby Club.

Mrs. Peacock knew that Mr. Boddy would keep his promise. She knew that the other guests would not.

35

So she was careful to lock all the Ball Room doors behind her before she began her yoga.

But she didn't see one of the guests spying on her through the keyhole as she hid a penny inside the piano.

Mrs. Peacock placed her head on the floor and kicked her black high heels up into the air.

She was standing on her head.

Now she could only see the brown rug and one black foot of the red sofa. And the next thing she heard was the sound of someone picking the lock of one of the Ball Room doors.

A pair of red sneakers tiptoed in and out of her line of vision.

Mrs. Peacock didn't say a word, however. And she didn't move. According to her yoga book, if she moved or spoke while in this position, the effect would be ruined.

The red sneakers tiptoed by again. Then they were gone.

For a moment, silence.

Then in the distance, Mrs. Peacock heard a quiet humming. The humming stopped. But there was a new sound to replace it. Someone was picking the lock of another one of the Ball Room doors.

Another pair of red sneakers tiptoed past. She heard a frustrated sigh. Then the red sneakers tiptoed past her again. And they were gone.

The silence didn't last long. Mrs. Peacock heard the sound of a third door being picked. Another pair of red sneakers tiptoed by. And by. And by. This guest seemed to be doing laps around the room.

Finally, she heard a tiny frustrated sigh.

Then she heard an electronic beep.

The red sneakers quickly tiptoed out of sight . . .

Just as Mrs. Peacock heard the fourth Ball Room door being picked.

This time, the sneakers that passed through her line of vision were blue.

A few minutes later, she heard a tiny cry of triumph.

Then the blue sneakers tiptoed by again, and were gone.

So was the penny, when Mrs. Peacock stopped standing on her head and checked inside the piano.

WHO STOLE MRS. PEACOCK'S PRICELESS PENNY?

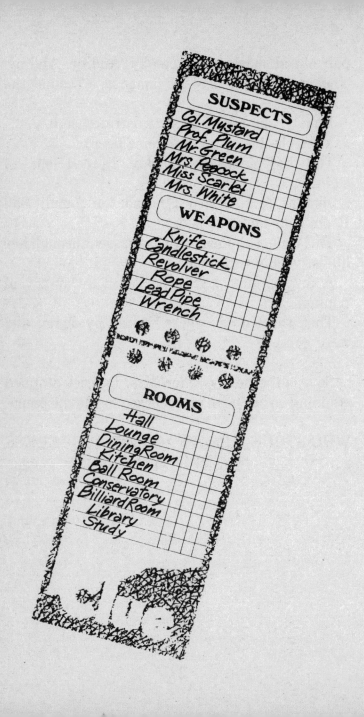

SOLUTION

COLONEL MUSTARD in the BALL ROOM

We know that Miss Scarlet and Mr. Green both were wearing red sneakers. So the guest with blue sneakers can't be either of them.

Mrs. White gave herself away when her electronic game beeped.

That leaves Mustard and Plum.

The forgetful professor had to leave the meeting early to search for his memory book. He didn't know about the priceless penny. So he's not a suspect.

It's Colonel Mustard.

Mrs. Peacock's not upset, however. She didn't hide the priceless penny in the piano. She hid the *worthless* penny there. For all his effort, Colonel Mustard simply stole his own penny back.

The priceless upside-down penny was underneath Mrs. Peacock's head.

6.
Seating Arrangements

MR. BODDY OPENED THE DOOR TO THE Study, stuck his head in, and announced proudly, "Lunch is served."

Inside the Study were the six members of Mr. Boddy's Gourmet Society. They all stood up eagerly.

"This way," Boddy called, leading his guests out of the Study and into the hallway. As he walked, Miss Scarlet hurried forward and slipped her arm through his.

"My dear," Mr. Boddy told her, "I think I've cooked up the greatest meal in the history of the Gourmet Society, if I do say so myself."

"I'm sure it's spectacular," Miss Scarlet said. She lowered her voice. "But if you don't want the meal to be ruined by bickering, please make sure that no two men sit next to each other, and no two women either!"

Boddy frowned. "Are you sure? Well, okay," he promised. "You've got it."

"And please," added Miss Scarlet, "whatever you do, don't seat me next to Mustard. Unless you want a murder on your hands!"

Miss Scarlet marched on past the Billiard Room with the other guests. Now Mrs. White caught up with her boss. "Maybe I shouldn't come to lunch at all," she told Mr. Boddy. "Maybe I should just help you serve."

"Nonsense," said Boddy. "It's your day off, I'll do all the serving, and besides — " He smiled warmly. "You're my favorite member of the entire Gourmet Society."

Mrs. White turned red with pleasure. Then she said, "Since you like me so much, please do me a big favor. Make sure not to seat me next to Peacock or Plum."

"All right," said the bewildered host. He turned left and walked past the Ball Room.

It was Colonel Mustard who caught up with him next. "I don't want to be a nuisance," Mustard muttered, "but would you mind not seating me next to Plum or Green? We're kind of in an argument and — "

"Say no more," Mr. Boddy said, waving his hand. I can't remember any more, Boddy added to himself.

But there was more.

Mrs. Peacock was next. She asked that she not be seated next to Green.

And Mr. Green asked that he not be seated next to Mustard.

Professor Plum almost forgot to make any request at all. But just as Mr. Boddy opened the door to the Dining Room, Plum remembered. "Would you mind not seating me next to Mr. Green or Mrs. White?" he asked.

Mr. Boddy nodded helplessly. His head was spinning.

He was the last one to walk into the Dining Room. But no one was sitting down at the circular oak dining table. They were all waiting for him to give the seating arrangements.

Oh, dear, thought Boddy desperately. His perfect gourmet meal was getting cold.

Think! he ordered himself. No two men sitting next to each other, no two women . . .

HURRY . . . BEFORE IT'S TOO LATE. . . . CAN YOU FIGURE OUT A SEATING ARRANGEMENT THAT WILL KEEP ALL THE GUESTS HAPPY? (RE-MEMBER — MR. BODDY WILL BE SERV-ING. HE WON'T BE SITTING AT THE TABLE.)

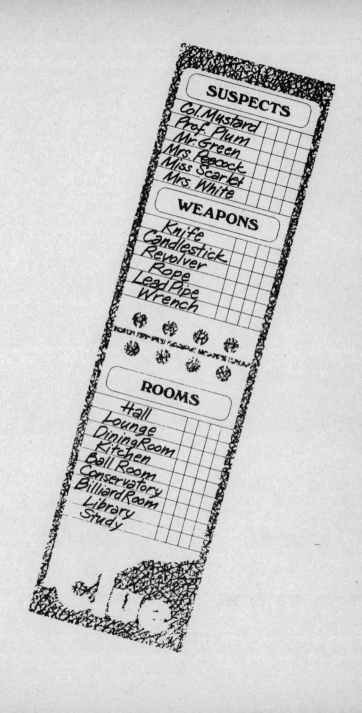

SOLUTION

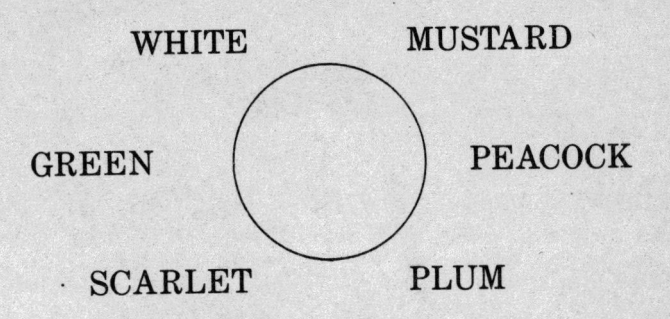

WHITE   MUSTARD

GREEN   PEACOCK

SCARLET   PLUM

7.
The Mystery at the Masked Ball

THE NIGHT SKY WAS CLEAR. THE MOON'S silver reflection shimmered on Boddy's Pond.

Nearby, on the lawn of the mansion, Mr. Boddy conducted a 300-piece orchestra as they played his favorite waltz, "Let's Waltz Walt's Waltz." Behind him, the Ball Room windows were open. The guests danced by, laughing gaily.

Mr. Boddy smiled proudly. What a success his masked ball was turning out to be! He glanced at his watch. Ten to ten. As soon as "Walt's Waltz" was done, he must award the $1,000 prize for best mask.

In the Ball Room, a man in a glittery purple mask waltzed with a woman in a gleaming blue mask. Suddenly Purple Mask stopped dancing. As a result, the two guests both toppled over in a heap.

"Sorry, sorry," said Purple Mask, helping Blue Mask to her feet.

Just then, a man in a glossy green mask cut between them. "May I cut in?" Green Mask asked Purple Mask.

"Please do!" said Blue Mask. "This man will be the death of me!"

Green Mask and Blue Mask waltzed off, leaving Purple Mask standing alone. He gazed about the Ball Room. Who could he dance with next? he wondered.

Then he saw her. A woman in a shiny scarlet mask, also standing alone. He hurried across the Ball Room toward her. On his way, he stepped on the toes of three masked guests.

Purple Mask and Scarlet Mask began waltzing happily. Until the other guests took revenge and stepped on *their* toes.

But still they kept dancing. And now they waltzed past the love seat. On the love seat lay the white envelope. The white envelope, they knew, contained the prize money. Purple Mask reached out and pocketed the envelope as they whirled by.

Suddenly, a man in a gleaming yellow mask came between them.

"May I cut in?" asked Yellow Mask. "I haven't had a chance to dance with this gorgeous woman even once tonight."

"Be my guest," said Purple Mask. Letting go of Scarlet Mask's dainty hand, he bowed low.

In return, Scarlet Mask curtsied even lower. In fact, she curtsied all the way down to the level of Purple Mask's pockets. And she stole the envelope.

Once again, Purple Mask was without a dancing

partner. He watched Green Mask waltzing with Blue Mask. Then he stepped up to them.

"Mind if I cut in?" he asked.

"Do the words 'I would rather die' suggest anything to you?" Blue Mask asked.

Purple Mask thought for a while, then shook his head. "Nope."

He grasped Blue Mask by the waist and waltzed her off across the floor.

At the same time, a woman with a beautiful white mask was waltzing with Green Mask.

"You dance divinely," said Green Mask.

"And you dance like an ox," said White Mask. "Kindly stop kicking my shins with your big shoes!"

There was a cry from the other side of the room. Blue Mask had bopped Purple Mask on the nose. Blue Mask and Purple Mask separated and began dancing with new partners.

White Mask and Green Mask kept on dancing. But suddenly, White Mask stopped short. As a result, White Mask and Green Mask toppled over in a heap.

"What's wrong?" Green Mask asked White Mask, when they were back on their feet.

"Nothing, nothing," muttered White Mask. "I just got distracted, that's all."

She didn't want to say what had distracted her. It was the sight of Yellow Mask stealing an envelope from Scarlet Mask.

"Sorry about that," White Mask now told Green Mask. She placed her arms around Green Mask's neck and resumed waltzing, all the while leading Green Mask toward Yellow Mask.

As she danced by, White Mask stole the envelope from Yellow Mask.

Then she danced Green Mask away.

But Green Mask wasn't as dumb as he seemed. Before the dance was done, Green Mask stole the envelope from White Mask.

The music stopped. Mr. Boddy entered beaming. "You all dance divinely," he said. "I'm sorry to stop you. But it's time to give out the prize for best mask."

He crossed to the sofa. But the envelope was, of course, missing.

"Oh, no," said Boddy. "Someone has taken the envelope with the prize money."

He stared at the guests. Six masks stared back at him silently.

"It's all right," Boddy said. "I'm not mad. I'm sure one of you took it just to make sure the money was kept safe for me. Now who has it?"

The six masked figures all pointed fingers at one another.

"There's no use pointing fingers," Boddy said. "I'm not mad at anyone. Besides, with all those masks on, I can't even tell who you are!"

"What a fool," muttered White Mask to herself. "Everyone's wearing their own color!"

Suddenly, Boddy began to weep. "None of my parties ever work out," he sobbed.

"Oh now, don't cry," said Green Mask. "I'm sure the envelope will turn up somewhere. Say, look!" He pointed to the floor at his feet. "Now I wonder where that came from?"

There lay the envelope.

"It came from your pocket," accused White Mask.

"That's a white lie," Green Mask fumed. "I just spotted it there this second."

Mr. Boddy, meanwhile, had picked up the envelope. "But it's empty," he said tearfully.

"Empty!" cried Green Mask. He snatched up the envelope and stared into it in surprise.

"Don't act so surprised," said White Mask. "You obviously pocketed the money, then discarded the envelope to throw us off the track."

"Search him!" cried Blue Mask.

The guests searched Green Mask. He didn't have the money.

"Or maybe," began Green Mask. He pointed an accusing finger at White Mask. "Maybe someone stole the money *out* of the envelope *before* anyone stole the envelope itself?"

"You may be right," admitted White Mask.

(And as a matter of fact, he *was* right!)

The masked guests all eyed each other suspiciously.

"I'm going to turn my back," Mr. Boddy said

49

tearfully. "On the count of three, I want whoever took that prize money to return it to me. If they don't . . . I'm going to go back to weeping!"

"Oh, please, Mr. Boddy," begged the masked guests. "No more crying!"

Mr. Boddy turned his back and crossed his arms and called out, "One . . . two . . ."

QUICK — WHO STOLE THE MONEY?

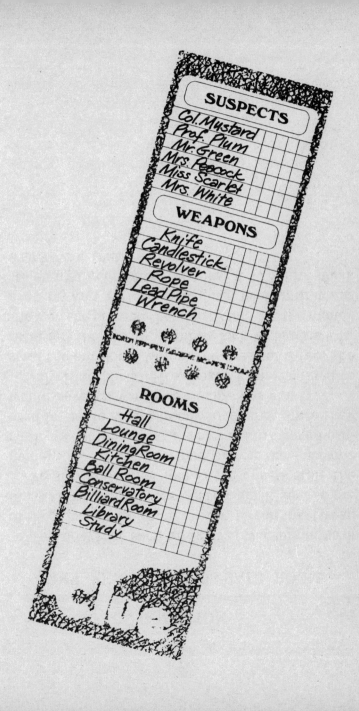

SOLUTION

MRS. PEACOCK in the BALL ROOM

We know that each guest was wearing a mask of the appropriate color. So Mr. Green was Green Mask, Miss Scarlet was Scarlet Mask, and so on.

We also know that one of the guests stole the money out of the envelope before the envelope itself was stolen. That guest wouldn't have bothered to try to steal the envelope later, since they would have known the envelope was empty.

Only Blue Mask (Mrs. Peacock) never tried to steal the envelope. Before the count of three, she returned the money. And as luck would have it, she won the prize for best mask and got the money back anyway. At least, she got it back until it was stolen by Green Mask who lost it to White Mask who — but that's another story.

8.
Farewell, Mrs. Peacock

ALL DAY LONG, THE WIND HOWLED. THE snow drifted down, down, down from the sky with no sign of stopping. Ever.

By evening, Mr. Boddy's mansion was completely blanketed with white. From the outside, the twelve-gabled house now looked like some giant wedding cake, sloppily covered with white icing.

And still the storm raged on.

Inside the mansion, Mr. Boddy, his maid, and his four guests all huddled in the Study before a cozy fire.

"We're snowbound for sure," Mrs. Peacock said. She stared glumly out the window as the thick flakes whirled endlessly down.

Boddy clapped his hands, trying to bring some cheer into the room. "Well," he said, "I can't imagine six people I'd prefer to be snowbound with. I mean, you're all such wonderful company. And we all get along so well."

"That's a laugh," said a strange, muffled voice.

"Who said that?" Boddy asked, looking around the room.

"I did," said the voice. It was impossible to tell whether the voice was male or female.

"I have an announcement to make," the voice continued. "It's a very, very important announcement, so you'd better listen up."

The guests were all peering around the Study, trying to figure out where the voice was coming from. It was strange — the voice seemed to be coming from the purple side chair.

"Here goes," said the voice. "At the stroke of midnight, Mrs. Peacock will die."

The guests gasped. Mrs. Peacock pulled up the purple seat cushion. Underneath was a loudspeaker. The guests started trailing the speaker wire. It led them out the Study door.

"I repeat," said the voice. "At the stroke of midnight, Mrs. Peacock will die."

Just outside the Study, on a chair, lay a tape recorder. Its spools turned slowly, menacingly.

Mr. Boddy reached for it.

"If you're thinking of turning me off, I'd think again," said the strange voice. "Mrs. Peacock's life is at stake, after all. I'm sure you want to hear everything I have to say."

Mr. Boddy's hand froze in midair. "This is the strangest thing I've ever seen," he murmured. "I'm sure this is all just some bizarre practical joke."

"It's no joke," said the taped voice. "But you don't have to take me seriously. Until midnight, that is. Because at midnight, Mrs. Peacock will die. Now is that serious enough for you?"

After a pause, the strange voice gave a small, strange chuckle. "I know what you're all thinking. That you'll find a way out. A way to save poor Peacock. But there's nothing you can do. I repeat, nothing. That's the beauty of my scheme. At the stroke of midnight tonight, Mrs. Peacock will die."

"Dust that thing for fingerprints," ordered Colonel Mustard.

"Right!" Mrs. White immediately wiped the machine thoroughly with a dust cloth.

"No, no, that's not what I meant," ranted Mustard. "Blast! You've just wiped away any fingerprints."

"Well," said Mr. Boddy. "We still have a pretty narrow group of suspects to choose from."

"What do you mean?" Mrs. Peacock asked nervously.

"The snowstorm," explained Boddy. "The roads are blocked everywhere. No one could get out to the mansion today. And no one who was here could leave. That means that the person who made this tape has to be . . ."

The guests all eyed one another nervously. It was Mrs. Peacock who finished Mr. Boddy's sentence. "One of us."

Mr. Boddy nodded. Mrs. Peacock shivered.

Then all the guests walked back into the Study and sat down.

"Why would anyone want to hurt you?" Mr. Boddy asked Mrs. Peacock.

Mrs. Peacock shook her head. "Oh, I'm sure everyone has their reasons. Everyone hates me."

"Nonsense!" cried the guests.

"No, it's true," Mrs. Peacock continued. "Just the other day, Mr. Green told me to drop dead."

"She wanted to wash my mouth out with soap for saying the word 'mud.' She said it was a dirty word," Green explained. "But I wasn't seriously suggesting that she — "

"And this morning," Mrs. Peacock interrupted, "Professor Plum told me if I touched his research papers again, he'd kill me," Mrs. Peacock continued. "Then Miss Scarlet said she'd shoot me because I threw out all her makeup. But — " Mrs. Peacock was crying now. "I can't help it if I'm the only one who knows that makeup is vulgar!"

Mr. Boddy patted her back. "All right, don't get yourself all worked up," he said. "They were mad at you, but I'm sure they wouldn't do anything really — "

"Then Mrs. White promised to klunk me with the Wrench if I didn't stop blackmailing her."

"Blackmailing her?" asked the stunned Mr. Boddy.

"Yes," confessed Mrs. Peacock. "You see, I

found out that Mrs. White once did a safecracking job."

"That's a filthy lie," yelled Mrs. White.

"But I was only blackmailing you to get the money back," continued Mrs. Peacock. "Then I was going to return the money to its rightful owner."

"That proves one thing," said Colonel Mustard. "Clearly I'm no longer a suspect. Because I have no motive."

Mrs. Peacock blew her nose. It sounded like a trombone. "Hardly," she said. "Why just this afternoon, the Colonel challenged me to a duel to the death."

All eyes were on Mustard now.

"But why?" asked Boddy.

"She was threatening me," said Mustard, his eyes flashing with anger. "She said that dueling is illegal."

"But it is," insisted Mrs. Peacock.

"She said she was going to go to the police," Mustard said, "if I ever fought another duel."

"And I will, too," said Mrs. Peacock. "For your sake. It's rude to break the law."

"Then I challenge you to a duel to the death!" shouted Mustard.

Mr. Boddy was scratching his chin. "Hmm. I guess we're back where we started — "

"In the Study," agreed Plum.

"No," said Boddy. "I mean, in terms of suspects. It could be any one of you."

"What time is it?" Mrs. Peacock asked.

Mr. Boddy checked his watch. "Eleven thirty-six. That means there are only twenty-four minutes left till midnight. I'm calling the police."

Colonel Mustard grabbed his arm. "What's the use? You said it yourself, the roads are blocked. They could never get here in time."

Mr. Boddy eyed the Colonel suspiciously. "It's still worth a try, isn't it?" He pulled his arm free and crossed the room to the phone.

"Hello?" he said into the receiver. "Hello? Hello?"

All of the guests watched Mr. Boddy as he slowly hung up. "Dead," he said quietly. "The line has gone dead."

"Don't say that word," Mrs. Peacock pleaded. "Please, from now on, nobody say that word."

"Listen," said Boddy. "I have some snowshoes in my room, and a snowmobile in the garage. I'll drive Mrs. Peacock to the police station where she can be safe."

Now it was Colonel Mustard's turn to be suspicious. "But how do we know you're not the one who made the tape? Maybe the snowmobile is part of your plan."

Boddy turned all the colors of his guests: red, green, blue, purple, yellow, and back to white. "You suspect *me*?"

Mustard shrugged. "We're all suspects, it seems to me. Everyone in this room. Except Mrs. Peacock herself."

"Fine then," said Boddy. "Mrs. Peacock can make the trip by herself. We'll all stay in the Study, and make sure no one leaves the room and tries to follow her."

The guests exchanged glances. It seemed like a good plan.

"Can I say something?" continued the strange tape, which had been playing silently all this time. "I would guess that by now you've thought of sending Mrs. Peacock off alone on the snowmobile. I can save you some time. I've taken the liberty of disposing of all the snowmobile's gasoline. Then I used the Wrench on its engine. The snowmobile is useless. Totally useless. You have until midnight, Mrs. Peacock. And then . . . farewell."

Mr. Boddy rushed up to his room, got the snowshoes, and rushed out into the blinding snow.

He returned moments later. "The tape's right," he said gravely. "The snowmobile's kaput."

Mrs. Peacock sagged. Mustard rushed to her side and helped her into the purple chair.

"Don't worry," he assured her. "We'll protect you. And we'll find the criminal who's responsible for this terrible torture."

"But how?" said Mrs. Peacock.

It was Mr. Boddy who answered first. "Why don't we start by frisking everyone for weapons?"

"Great idea," said Mustard. "But we can't frisk me because I'm terribly ticklish. No! Please!"

But the guests were slowly approaching Mustard in a circle. They all frisked him at once.

"Ha-ha-he-he-ho-ho!" roared Mustard. "Oh, stop! Please! Stop!"

But the guests didn't stop until they had found Mustard's Revolver. Which they handed to Mr. Boddy.

"I always carry it," said the Colonel, turning yellow. "In case I have to fight a duel."

"Were you planning on fighting a duel with Mrs. Peacock at midnight?" asked Plum.

"You dare to accuse me?" roared Mustard. "I challenge you to a duel!"

But he no longer had his Revolver.

The other guests coughed up the remaining weapons.

"I'm going to get rid of these," Boddy said, opening the Study window. Wet icy snow blasted into the room. One after another, he flung the six weapons out the window. Beginning with the Wrench, the Revolver, and the Rope, weapon after weapon disappeared into the dark. None of the weapons made a sound. The blanket of snow cushioned each weapon's fall.

Mr. Boddy shut the window and looked at the clock on the wall. "Eight minutes left."

The guests listened to the sound of the ticking. Each tick sounded like a threat.

"Seven," said all the guests at once. Their eyes were glued to the clock as it ticked relentlessly around once again.

"Six minutes!" the guests cried.

Five minutes to twelve. . . . Four. . . . Three.

"Don't worry, Mrs. Peacock," Mr. Boddy said, his own voice trembling. "Nothing will happen to you. I'll see to that."

"Me, too," agreed Plum. He slapped Mrs. Peacock on the back. She started to cough. "Sorry," he said.

"Two minutes to go!" cried the guests.

The ticking seemed endless.

"One!" shouted the guests.

All eyes were frozen on the minute hand of the wall clock. Finally, the hand nudged forward.

Now everyone looked around wildly.

It was midnight. Who was the murderer?

The Study window shattered.

All heads turned in terror.

Outside, in the raging snowstorm, stood a figure cloaked in snow. Thanks to the snow, they couldn't tell who it was.

But the white figure held the Revolver. That much they could see. And the Revolver was pointed right at Mrs. Peacock.

The guests all stared at one another in amazement. Then Mr. Boddy screamed. "There are only six of us in the room." He pointed at the figure with the Revolver. "That's one of us!"

The figure only laughed. "Correct, Mr. Boddy," said the guest in a disguised voice. The voice of the tape.

There was a click. The figure removed the safety latch on the Revolver. "You've solved the puzzle. But a little late, I'm afraid. Farewell, Mrs. Peacock," said the snowy figure.

And then the figure fired.

WHO KILLED MRS. PEACOCK?

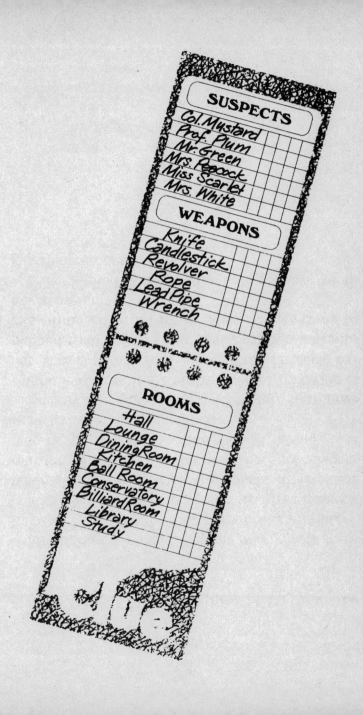

SOLUTION

MISS SCARLET outside the STUDY with the REVOLVER

Mr. Boddy, his maid, and his *four* guests were huddled in the Study. One person was missing.

Miss Scarlet was mentioned by Mrs. Peacock when she was reviewing the guests' motives for murder. But Miss Scarlet was the only suspect who never spoke. She didn't speak because she wasn't there. She was outside.

Luckily, Mr. Boddy had the foresight to remove the bullets from the Revolver before throwing it out the window. And when Mrs. Peacock explained that she still had Miss Scarlet's makeup, and promised to return it, Miss Scarlet came to her senses.

"Ah," sighed Boddy. "Like I always say, we all get along so beautifully!"

9.
A Mysterious Meeting

IT WAS THE MIDDLE OF THE NIGHT. THE only light in the Lounge was a patch of moonlight that shone through the window.

By this dim light, one could just barely see the dark forms of two of Mr. Boddy's guests who sat across from each other.

"It's a crazy plan," said one.

"But it will work," said the other. "I promise you."

"Let me get this straight," said the first guest. "I commit a murder for you?"

"Right," said the second guest.

"Now, I commit this murder while you're away."

"Right, so I have an alibi," said the second guest.

"Then," the first guest continued, "you commit a murder for me."

"While *you're* away." The second guest smiled patiently.

"That way, *I* have an alibi," continued the first guest.

"You've got it now," said the second guest.

"And then — " began the first.

"And then," continued the second guest, "no one will suspect either one of us, because neither one of us will have a motive in the crime we committed."

There was a long silence.

Then the first guest answered. "Agreed."

One week later . . .

One week later, the guests were all spending the weekend at Boddy's mansion. All except for Mr. Green and Mrs. Peacock, that is. Saturday morning began with a scream.

Miss Scarlet had found Professor Plum lying face down, the Wrench lying beside him. Mr. Boddy quickly gathered all the guests, trying to get to the bottom of the crime.

As it turned out, only two guests were known to have a motive for the attack: Green and Peacock. But neither Peacock nor Green were at the mansion during the crime. Strange!

The crime went unsolved. And . . .

One week later . . .

One week later, the guests were all staying at Boddy's mansion. All except for Plum, that is, who was still mad about getting klonked with the

Wrench. And except for Mrs. Peacock and Colonel Mustard, who were away on business.

The morning began with another scream. Mr. Green found Miss Scarlet lying face down on the floor of the Study, the Lead Pipe lying on the floor beside her.

Mr. Boddy held another meeting. As it turned out, the only guests with motives were Mustard and Peacock. But Peacock and Mustard weren't at the mansion at the time. Strange!

The crime went unsolved. Until . . .

One week later . . .

One week later, all the guests were gathered at Boddy's for the weekend. All except for Plum and Scarlet, who were both mad about getting bonked on the head. And for Green and Peacock, who were away on business.

The morning began with a scream. Mr. Boddy had found Mrs. White, lying face down on the Kitchen floor. The Candlestick lay on the black and white tiles beside her.

The only guest with a motive was Mr. Green. But Green was out of town. Strange!

"Very strange," agreed Mrs. White, her voice muffled by the black and white tile floor.

Mr. Boddy did a double take. "Mrs. White! You're talking! You're not dead! You're all right!"

He turned her over. Her eyes were still closed. He began pinching her cheeks. "Tell me you're all right! Tell me you're all right!"

Mrs. White's eyes fluttered open. "I would be all right if you would stop pinching my cheeks."

"Please, Mrs. White," said Mr. Boddy. "Think! Who would want to hurt you like this?"

"I know exactly who it was," said the maid. "A few weeks ago, I passed by the Lounge. The lights were out. But I heard voices. I put my eye to the keyhole, but I couldn't see a thing."

"But then how can you — " began Boddy.

"Wait," said Mrs. White, "I'm not finished yet. I listened at the door. And I overheard two guests planning a strange crime. For two weeks now, I've been trying to figure out whose voices I heard. Then tonight, I figured out who one of the voices belonged to. I approached that guest with my suspicion and, well, you can see what happened."

"What?" asked Boddy.

"The guest bopped me one," Mrs. White said irritably, before her eyes closed again.

"Who was it?" Boddy asked her eagerly. "Who hit you?"

"It was — "

But Mrs. White had passed out again before she could name her attacker.

WHO ATTACKED MRS. WHITE? WHO WAS THE OTHER PLOTTER?

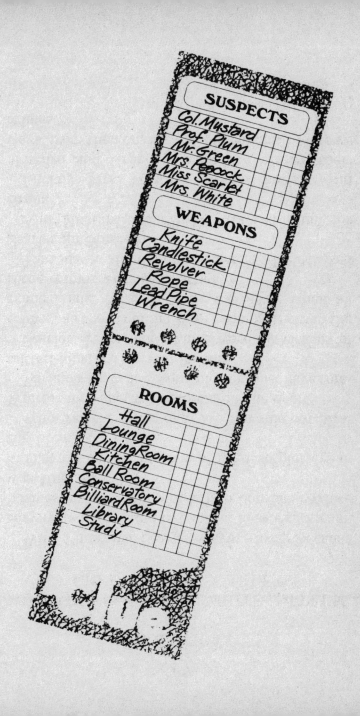

SOLUTION

MUSTARD attacked MRS. WHITE and PLUM. GREEN attacked SCARLET.

With Plum and Scarlet staying away because they were angry, and Green and Peacock away on business, the only guest left to bop Mrs. White was Mustard.

That means he was one of the two plotters in the Lounge.

Who was the other one? We can rule out Mrs. White, since she was listening at the door.

We know that the second plotter must have committed Mustard's crime for him.

Scarlet, Plum, and White were all victims of crimes, so they couldn't have been partners in the crime trade. Mrs. Peacock was away when all three crimes were committed.

That leaves Mr. Green as the one who attacked Scarlet for Mustard.

And Mustard must have attacked Plum for Green.

Luckily, Mrs. White recovered quickly. And Mustard and Green promised to change their ways: from then on, they would commit their own crimes.

10.
Mr. Boddy Passes On

Mrs. WHITE FROWNED BITTERLY AS she wheeled her silver serving cart toward the Dining Room. But once she was inside the room, she put on a bright smile.

Here were all of Mr. Boddy's guests, sitting around the Dining Room table, laughing merrily.

It wasn't until the guests looked away that Mrs. White's bitter frown returned. Then she started smiling again and began serving the ice cream.

Mr. Boddy waited while his guests were served first.

"Whoopee! Dessert!" he cried. Then he sighed a happy sigh. "Gosh, it just doesn't get any better than this." He beamed at his guests.

"It's great to see you in such a jolly mood," Miss Scarlet told her host.

It was true. Mr. Boddy was feeling jolly. He was feeling more jolly than he had ever felt before. So it was probably a good thing that he didn't know that he would be dead by morning.

"Why shouldn't I be jolly?" Boddy continued. "Wonderful company, wonderful food, and wonderful service." He turned to thank Mrs. White just as she served him his ice cream. As a result, his shoulder collided with her arm and sent a glob of ice cream flying in the air.

The ice cream landed with a *splat* on the head of Mrs. Peacock, the guest to the left of Boddy.

"Playing with your food!" she cried. "How rude!"

"I'm so sorry," insisted Mrs. White, wiping the top of Peacock's head with a napkin. Mrs. White looked very jolly as she wheeled her serving cart out of the room.

At the same time, Mr. Green leaned over and placed his mouth right next to the ear of the guest on Mrs. Peacock's left. "Would Boddy be mad if Plum, Scarlet, and I went into town?" he whispered. "Pass it on!"

Unfortunately, Mr. Green whispered too softly. The guest didn't hear well and whispered to Mrs. Peacock, "Green says Boddy would be glad if we all laughed and jumped up and down. Pass it on!"

Unfortunately, the guest didn't whisper loudly enough. And Mrs. Peacock whispered to Mr. Boddy, "Would you really be glad if we all rolled around on the ground?"

"Oh, how thoughtful of you to ask," exclaimed Boddy. Unfortunately, Mrs. Peacock hadn't whispered loudly enough. Boddy whispered to the guest on his right, "I'm still sad because I just sold my old hound."

The guest looked at Boddy, surprised. Then the guest whispered to the next guest, "Boddy's sad because someone stole his old hound."

The next guest looked surprised and whispered to Mr. Green, "Mr. Boddy's afraid someone will steal his gold clown."

Mr. Green looked surprised and whispered to the next guest, "Boddy is afraid someone will steal his solid gold crown."

This last guest heard perfectly well. But kept silent until —

Later that night . . .

Later that night, after everyone was asleep, the last guest snuck into Boddy's room. The guest flicked on the light.

"Okay, Mr. Boddy," said the guest, aiming a Revolver at the host. "Hand it over!"

Boddy was perplexed. He was also sleepy. "Am I dreaming?" he asked. "Pinch me, would you?"

"Never mind that. Just hand it over!"

"Okay," said Boddy in a shaky voice. "But I can't sleep without my blankie." Mr. Boddy handed over his blanket.

The guest threw the blanket to the floor. "Not your blanket, you fool! The solid gold crown."

"The what?" Mr. Boddy asked meekly.

"The solid gold crown!"

"Maybe *you're* dreaming," suggested Mr. Boddy. "Because I don't know what you're talking about."

The Revolver jabbed into Boddy's rib cage. "I said hand over the solid gold crown."

"Ow!" said Mr. Boddy. "Thanks! That proves I'm awake. But I still don't know what solid gold crown you're talking about."

The guest with the Revolver sighed angrily. "The solid gold crown Mr. Green says you're afraid someone will steal."

"Ah," said Mr. Boddy. But then he shook his head. "I'm still stumped."

"Look," said the guest. "I'll tear this room apart if I have to."

When Mr. Boddy didn't answer, the guest began to do just that. The guest started tearing the room apart. "Stop!" cried Boddy, getting out of bed.

He rushed at the guest. They struggled. And in the struggle, the Revolver went off.

Boddy dropped to the floor, dead.

"Serves you right," said the bitter guest. "You should have just given me the solid gold crown."

WHO KILLED MR. BODDY?

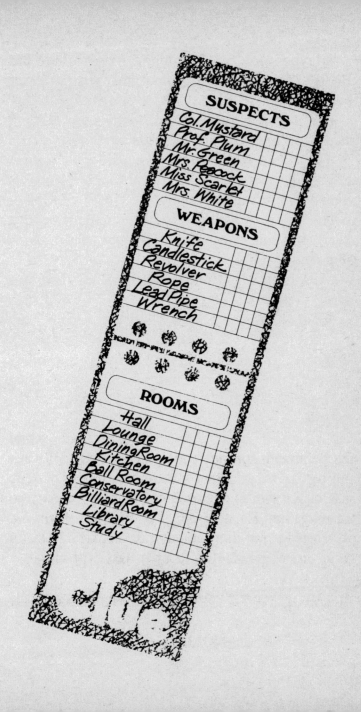

SOLUTION

COLONEL MUSTARD with the REVOLVER

When Mr. Green first whispered to the murderer, he whispered about Plum and Scarlet. So we know that the murderer isn't Plum, Scarlet, or Green. And it's not Mrs. Peacock, who was sitting to the murderer's right. Mrs. White left the room and never heard the whispering. That leaves only Mustard.

NOTES

NOTES

NOTES

NOTES

NOTES

HI ♥

Hi ♥

Hi ♥

Love ♥

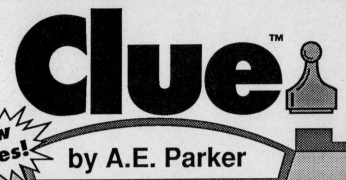